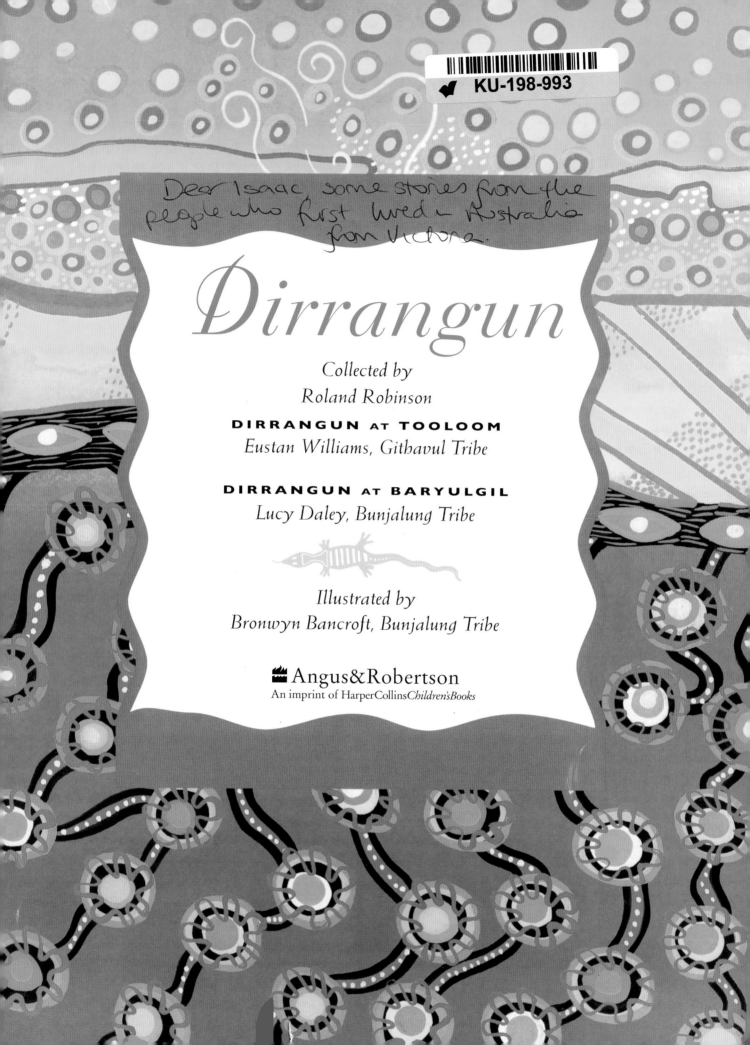

Dear Isaac, some stories from the people who first lived in Australia from Victoria.

# Dirrangun

Collected by
Roland Robinson

**DIRRANGUN** at **TOOLOOM**
Eustan Williams, Githavul Tribe

**DIRRANGUN** at **BARYULGIL**
Lucy Daley, Bunjalung Tribe

Illustrated by
Bronwyn Bancroft, Bunjalung Tribe

Angus&Robertson
An imprint of HarperCollins*Children'sBooks*

# Dirrangun at Tooloom

*Related by Eustan Williams,*
*Githavul Tribe*

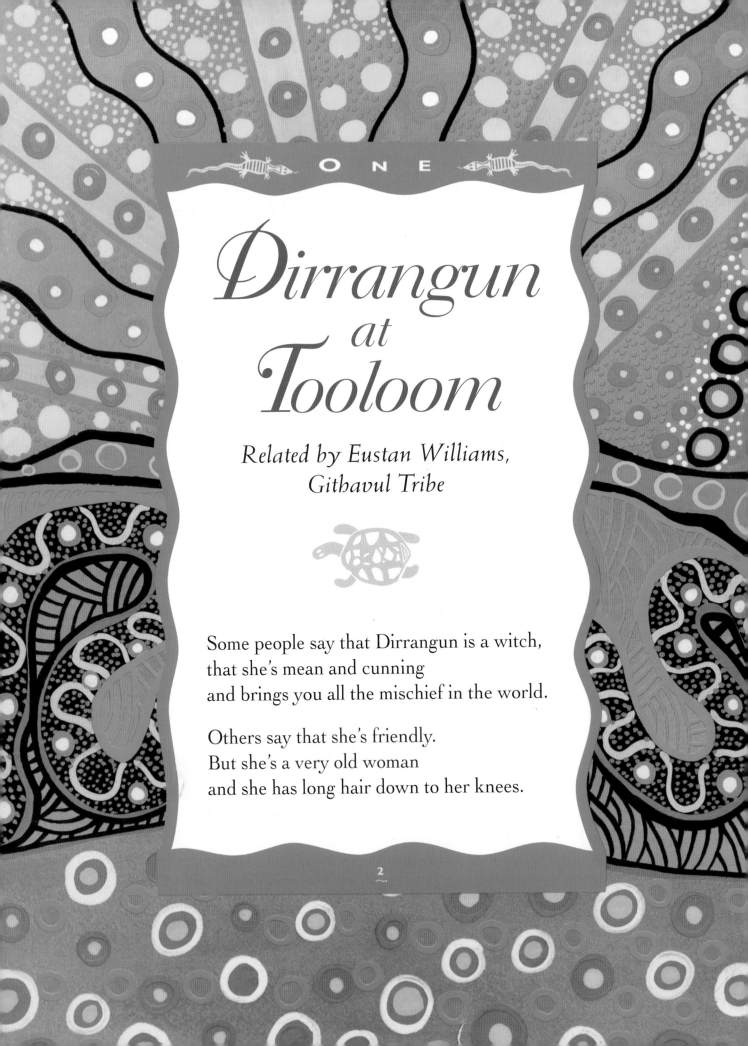

Some people say that Dirrangun is a witch,
that she's mean and cunning
and brings you all the mischief in the world.

Others say that she's friendly.
But she's a very old woman
and she has long hair down to her knees.

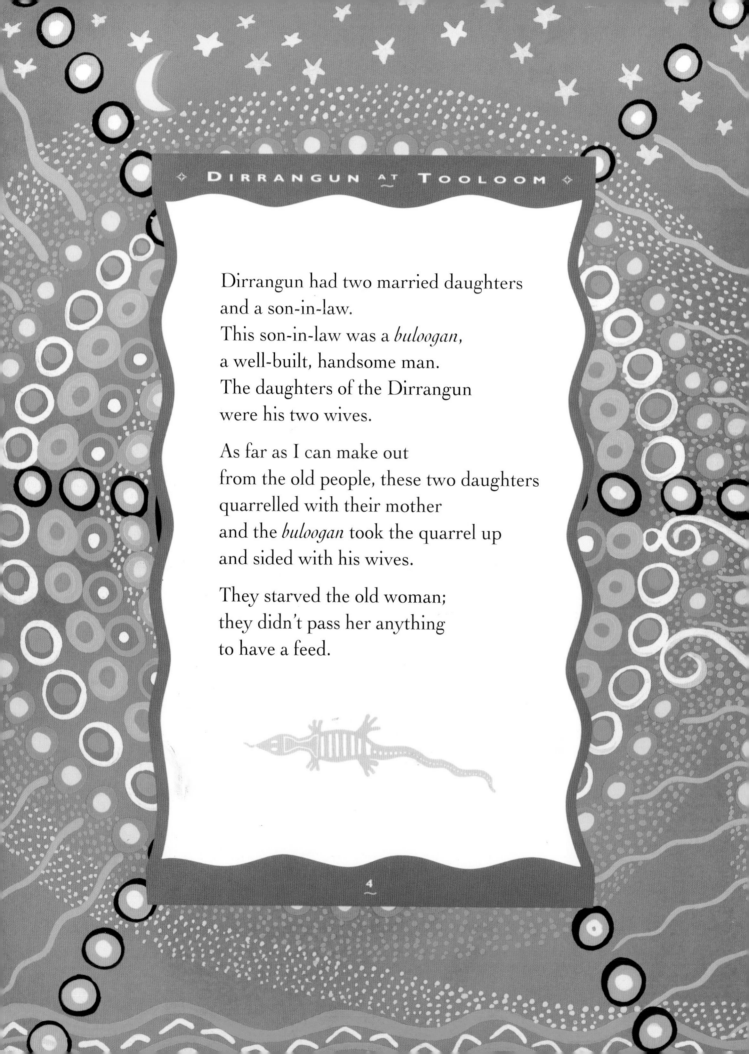

Dirrangun had two married daughters
and a son-in-law.
This son-in-law was a *buloogan*,
a well-built, handsome man.
The daughters of the Dirrangun
were his two wives.

As far as I can make out
from the old people, these two daughters
quarrelled with their mother
and the *buloogan* took the quarrel up
and sided with his wives.

They starved the old woman;
they didn't pass her anything
to have a feed.

Dirrangun's camp was under a big fig-tree,
here at this waterfall which is
the source of the Clarence River.

There was a basin here,
a hollow in the rock,
which contained the water.
Dooloomi was the name of the pool.
It was the *jurraveel*, the home
of the spirit of the water.
Tooloom now is the white man's name
for this waterfall.
Tooloom is the nearest he could get
to saying Dooloomi.

While the son-in-law and his two wives
were out hunting and gathering food,
Dirrangun drained the water out of the pool
with a bark coolamon.

Some people say that she put the fire out,
too, so that there was no fire in the world.

When the *buloogan* and his two wives
came home in the evening,
there was no water.
The two wives were running about
all over the place looking for water.
But there was no water.
Dirrangun had put leaves and bark
over the empty basin hole in the rock
so that the place was hidden.

For two or three days
the *buloogan* and his wives
could not get a drink of water.

Dirrangun was pretending to cry for them.
Some people say that Dirrangun
was sitting on this coolamon of water
in her camp, hiding it.

These people say that when the *buloogan*
found this out, he got angry and cried,
'Well, you're not going to have
all the water! I'll let it out!'
He thrust his spear into that coolamon,
*biggi* we call it, and let it out.

Others say that when Dirrangun,
the *buloogan* and his two wives went
to sleep, the *buloogan*'s two dogs,
who were thirsty,
found the water which Dirrangun
had hidden in the coolamon.

You see those two mountains?
They were called Dillalea
and Kalloo-Guthun.
They are named after those two dogs.

In the night those two dogs returned
to the camp of the *buloogan*
and stood over him.
And the water dripped from their mouths.
When the *buloogan* felt this he woke up.
He followed the two dogs back
to where Dirrangun was asleep
with the hidden water.

When the *buloogan* saw where
the water was hidden, he was angry.
He made a big rain, a big pour-down rain.
The hollow rock-basin began to fill.
The water rose and rose and backed up
where this creek is now.

Some say that when the water began to rise
Dirrangun climbed into the fig-tree
and made a platform in the boughs.
But the water rose and swept her
and the fig-tree away
and left this hollow beneath these cliffs
where the waterfall is now.

Dirrangun was holding on to the fig-tree
as she was swept away.
She was swept over the second fall,
which we call Ngalumbeh.
At the bottom of this fall
she was whirled round and round,
still holding on to the fig-tree,
in a whirlpool for half a day.

The water was getting stronger and stronger.
The *buloogan* had cursed the water
to make it unmanageable.
It took her and the fig-tree away
down into the Clarence River.
From time to time Dirrangun
would sit in the torrent
with her legs wide apart
trying to block the water, but each time
the flood would bear her away.

Where the South River
comes into this river,
Dirrangun sat with her legs outspread.
The water rose and went up
and made the South River.
There she sat until the flood rose
and swept her and the fig-tree on again.

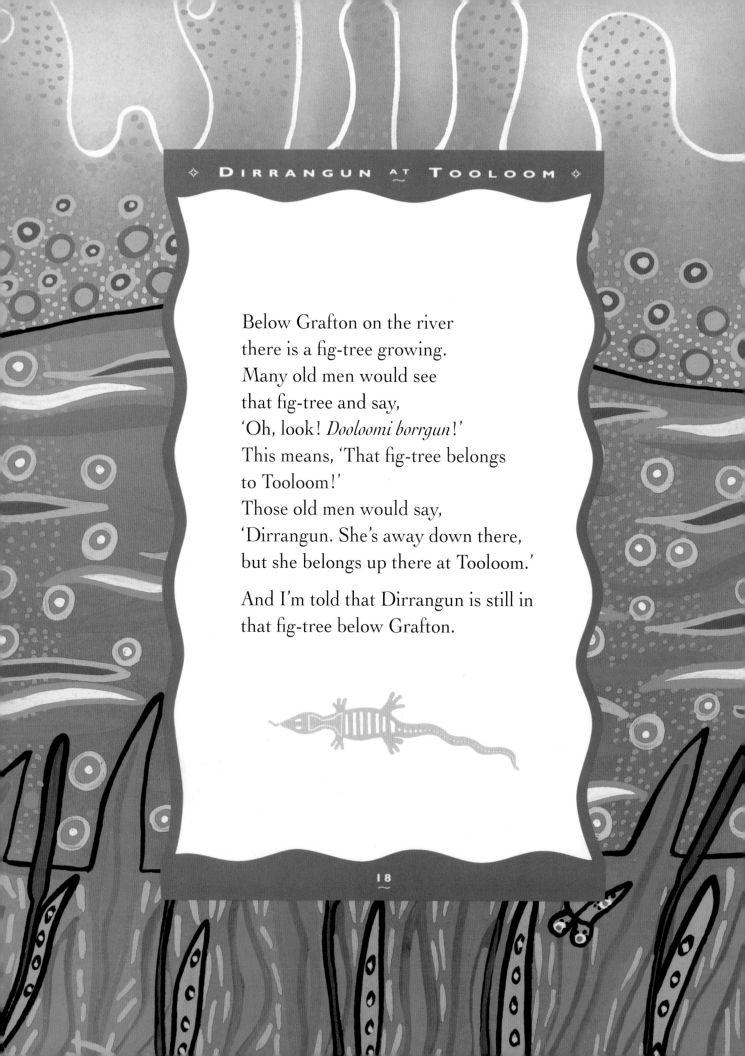

Below Grafton on the river
there is a fig-tree growing.
Many old men would see
that fig-tree and say,
'Oh, look! *Dooloomi borrgun*!'
This means, 'That fig-tree belongs
to Tooloom!'
Those old men would say,
'Dirrangun. She's away down there,
but she belongs up there at Tooloom.'

And I'm told that Dirrangun is still in
that fig-tree below Grafton.

# T W O

# Dirrangun
### at
# Baryulgil

*Related by Lucy Daley,*
*Bunjalung Tribe*

Somewhere in the mountains
near Tooloom,
in those forests of tall trees,
somewhere in those mountains
hidden by drifting mists,
the old woman Dirrangun
kept hidden her sacred spring.

This old woman didn't want anyone
to know where the water was.
It was good water and
she used to get it herself.
But one day she was sick.
And there was a young man
called a *bulagaan*.

He was a very well-built young man,
he was handsome.
She asked this *bulagaan*
if he would go and get the water.
She sent him up to this secret spring
to get the water.

She had to direct him and tell where it was.
So the *bulagaan* set off into the mountains
to get some of the water in a bark coolamon.

When the *bulagaan* got to the water
he found that Dirrangun
had dammed the water up.

The *bulagaan* broke the dam
and the water started to run away.

When Dirrangun saw the water coming,
she started to try and dam the water.
But the water broke through them.

And at last the water came down
and went into the sea
which we call in the language *Burraga*.

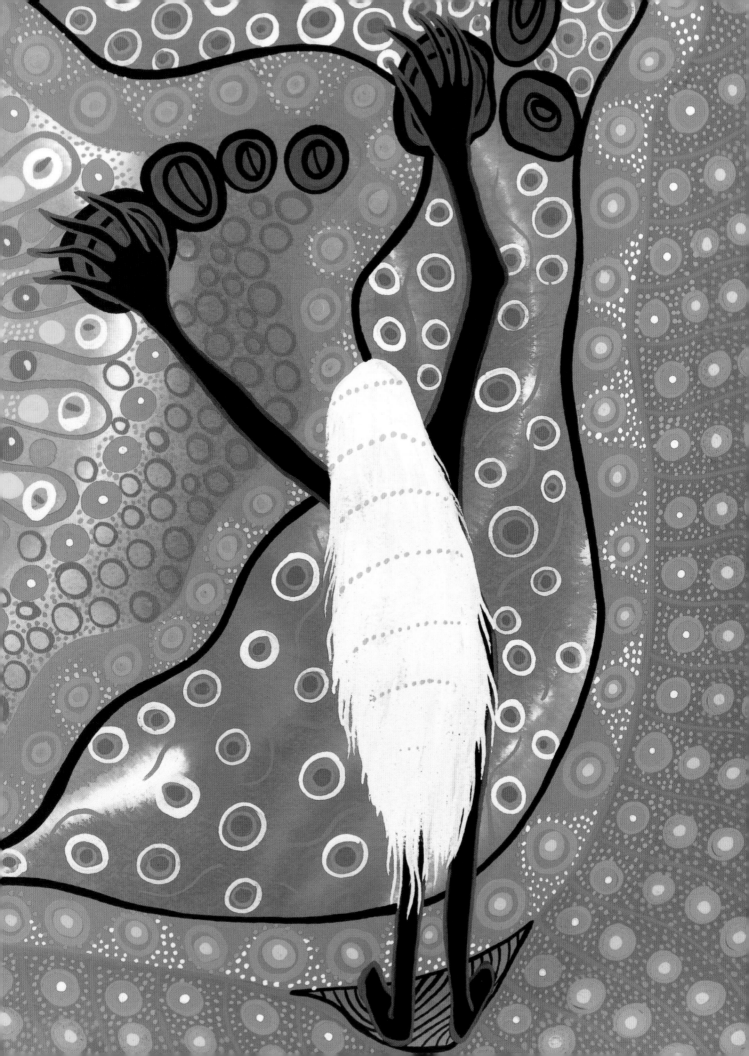

That's how this river, the Clarence,
came to be here.
This Mount Ogilvie here,
that's one of the dams Dirrangun made.

The gorge down below Baryulgil here
is the place of the last dam
that Dirrangun made.
But the water broke through.

When the water got down to Yamba,
Dirrangun realised that she couldn't stop it,
so she cursed it and made it salt
so that no one could drink it.

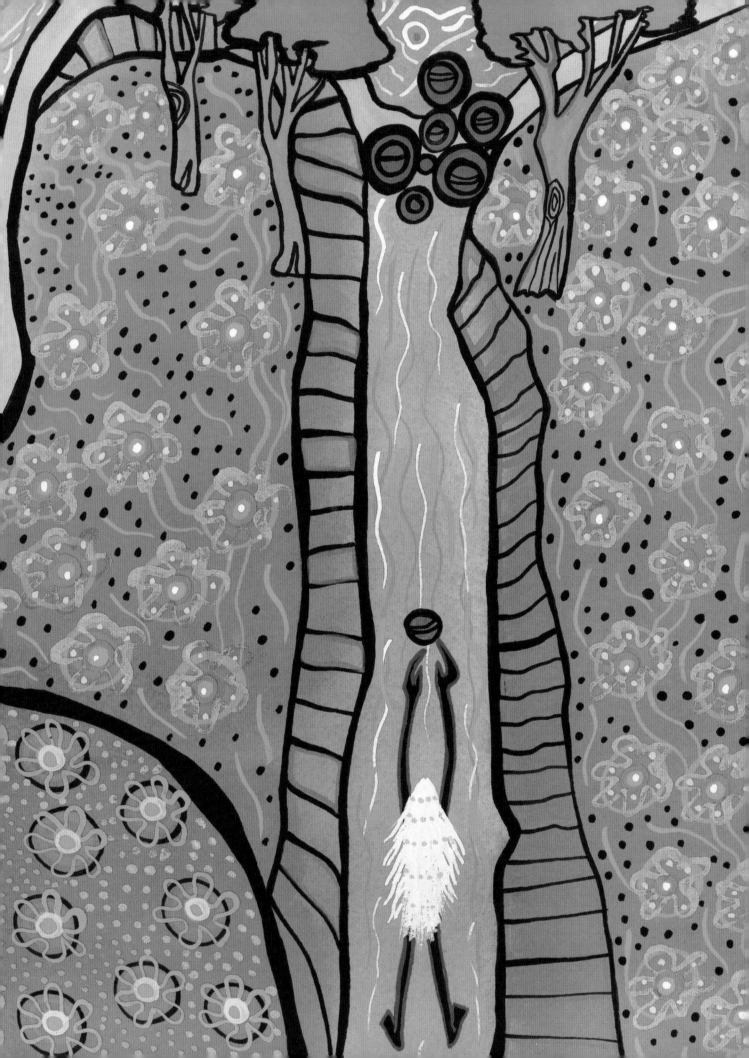

Somewhere in the mouth of the Clarence
is the last stand of Dirrangun
as she tried to stop the water.

She threw herself in front of the water
to try and stop it with herself,
but the water just rushed over her and
she was turned into stone.

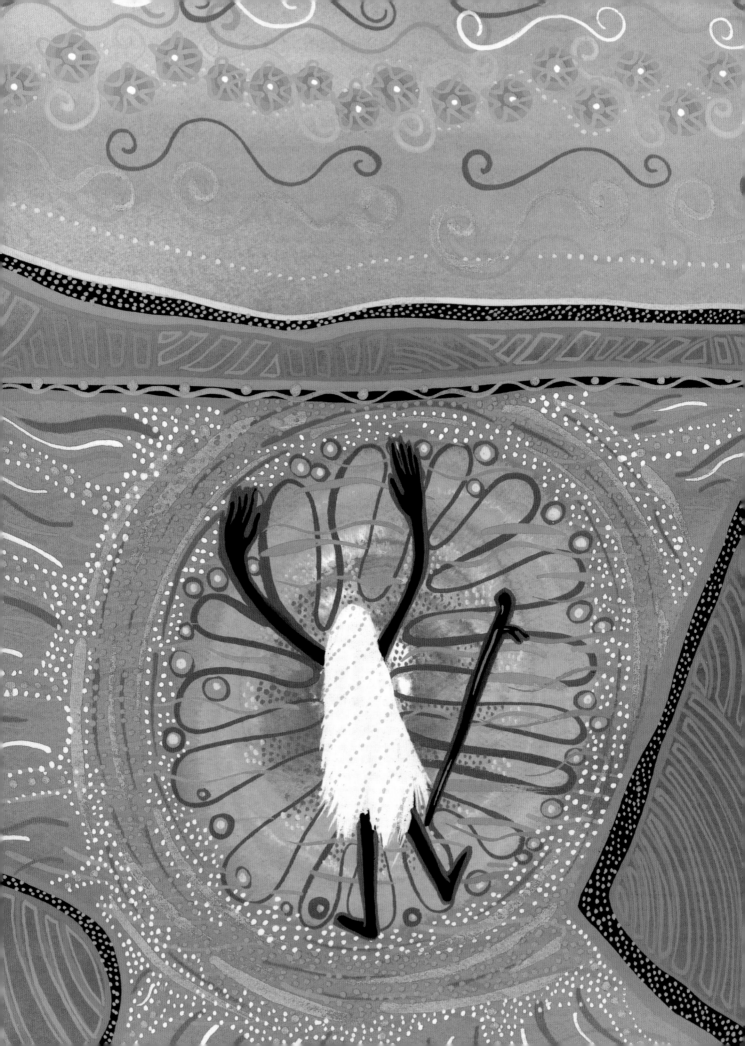

**Angus&Robertson**
An imprint of HarperCollins*Children'sBooks* Australia

First published in Australia in *The Nearest the White Man Gets*
by Hale & Iremonger in 1989
This edition published in Australia in 1994
by HarperCollins*Publishers* Pty Limited
ABN 36 009 913 517
harpercollins.com.au

Stories collected from Eustan Williams and Lucy Daley by Roland Robinson
Text copyright © The Estate of the late Roland Robinson 1989, 1994
Illustrations copyright © Bronwyn Bancroft, 1994

**HarperCollins*Publishers***
Level 13, 201 Elizabeth Street, Sydney NSW 2000, Australia
Unit D1, 63 Apollo Drive, Rosedale, Auckland 0632, New Zealand

ISBN 978 0 7322 9533 2

The Australian Children's Classics logo designed by Matt Stanton
Colour reproduction by Graphic Print Group, South Australia
Printed and bound in China by RR Donnelley

5 4 3          17 18